Polly Alakija

Help, help! Where has that goat gone?

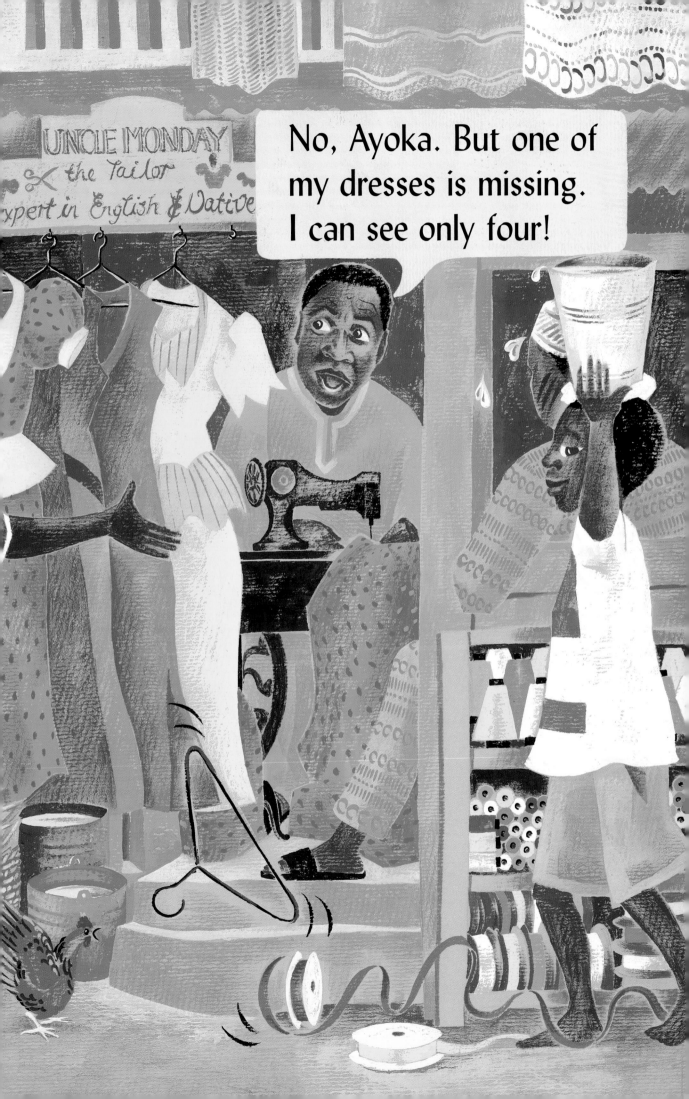

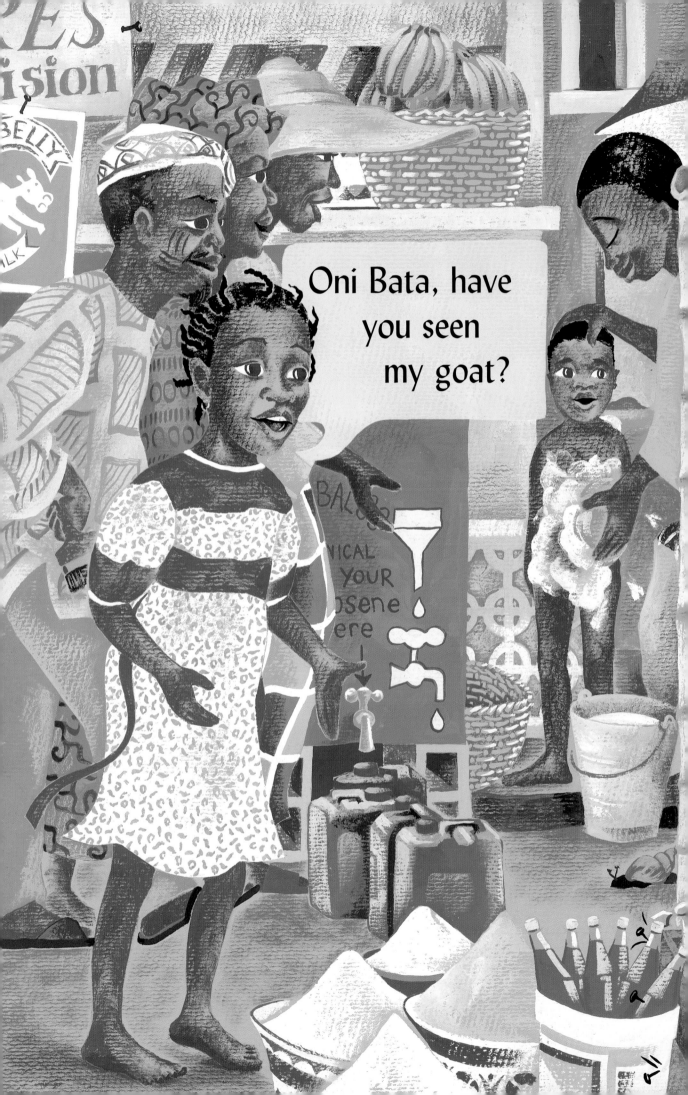

Yoruba People

Ayoka is a Yoruba girl from Nigeria. The Yorubas are one of the largest tribes there. They are well known for their music, dance and art. You may have seen a woodcarving from Oyo or a bronze sculpture from Benin in a museum. Some Yorubas have tribal markings on their faces, though this is not as common as it used to be. Family is very important to Yorubas and even distant relatives help each other out. People who do a lot for the community may be awarded a chieftaincy title. Yorubas love to laugh and enjoy themselves; they are said to be some of the happiest people on earth!

Yoruba people have moved to many corners of the world. Wherever they go, their culture follows. If you look closely, you may see someone selling yams in London, or you may hear the beat of talking drums in New York.

Behind every Yoruba name there is a story:
'Ayo' means joy; Ayoka is someone who brings us joy.
'Iya' means mother; Iyaolomon is a mother of many children.
If you meet someone called Taiwo or Kehinde, you know from their name that they are a twin.

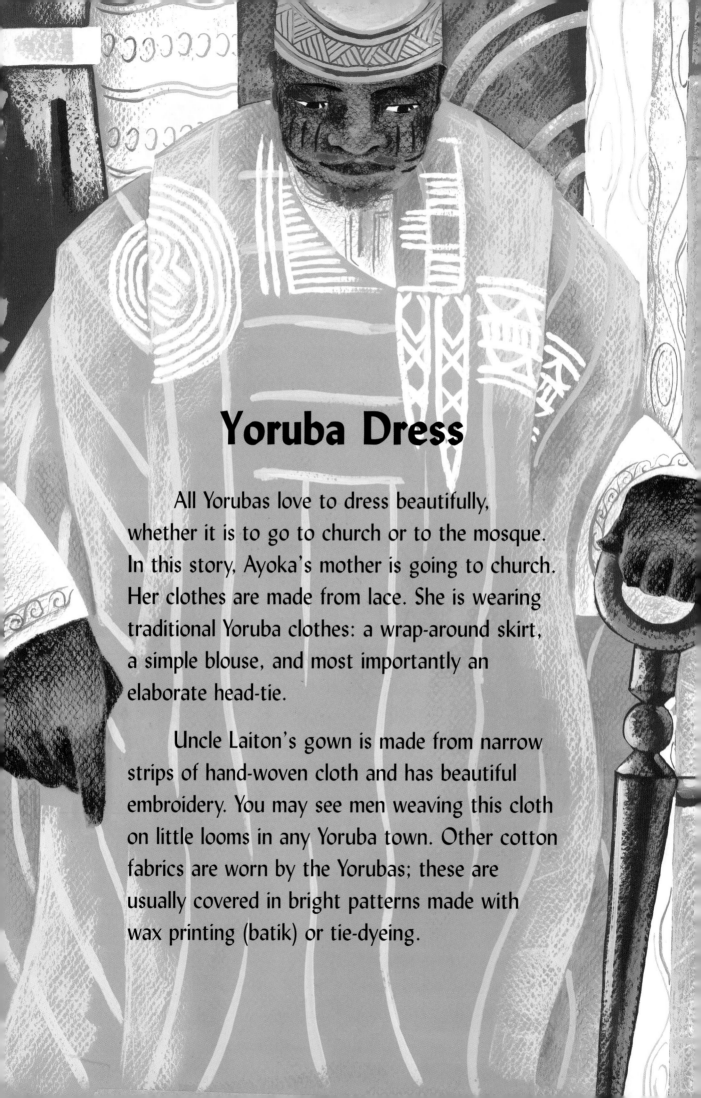

Yoruba Dress

All Yorubas love to dress beautifully,
whether it is to go to church or to the mosque.
In this story, Ayoka's mother is going to church.
Her clothes are made from lace. She is wearing
traditional Yoruba clothes: a wrap-around skirt,
a simple blouse, and most importantly an
elaborate head-tie.

Uncle Laiton's gown is made from narrow
strips of hand-woven cloth and has beautiful
embroidery. You may see men weaving this cloth
on little looms in any Yoruba town. Other cotton
fabrics are worn by the Yorubas; these are
usually covered in bright patterns made with
wax printing (batik) or tie-dyeing.

Yoruba Language

In towns, most people speak English and Yoruba. Greetings are very important, and young people must always show respect for their elders in the way they greet them. This is why Ayoka must address people correctly, starting with Oga (Sir), Baba (Uncle or Mr), Oni (the title given to a trader), Uncle or Auntie. This does not mean Auntie Wemimo really is her auntie, but it is a sign of respect, and friendship.

1 → 10 in Yoruba

1
eni

2
eji

3
eta

4
rin

5
aarun

6
eefa

7
eeje

8
eejo

9
eesan

10
eewa

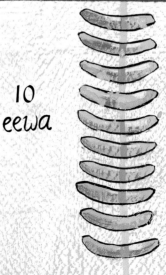

Saying 'Hello!' in Yoruba

E kaaro – Good morning
E kaasan – Good afternoon
E ku irole – Good (early) evening
E ku ale – Good (late) evening

Everyday life for Ayoka

Ayoka lives in Ibadan, in the Ademola compound. Several families, or lots of people from one big family, share one compound. Everyone is happy to help each other out, and even children, when they get back from school, have their chores to do. They look after younger brothers or sisters, sweep the compound, draw water from the well, or help prepare food. Ayoka's job was to look after the goat!

Most people in Ibadan are Yoruba. Some are Christian and some are Muslim. There are many different churches and mosques. Even in the markets you may come across a small church or a small quiet corner where Muslims pray. There are many public holidays to celebrate the main Christian and Muslim holy days. Children are happy to have time off school but they also learn to respect each other's religion.

Visiting the Market

The market in Ayoka's town is a very busy, hot and noisy place. In every last corner, someone is selling something. Food is always being cooked. Outside Ayoka's compound Mama Kudi sells 'boli'. This is roasted plantain. You can also see a lady making 'akara'. This is fried bean cake, usually eaten as breakfast. Outside Mama Put's 'buka' (a little restaurant) some ladies are pounding yam.

Every item on sale is beautifully displayed, even if it is just a cleaning brush. Tropical fruits are piled high, groundnuts bagged to make little pyramids, smoked catfish curled up on sticks. But look out for those giant snails (a real delicacy) because they refuse to stay put in their basket! Wherever you go, there are little goats. You may think they are lost, but everyone knows exactly which goat is theirs!

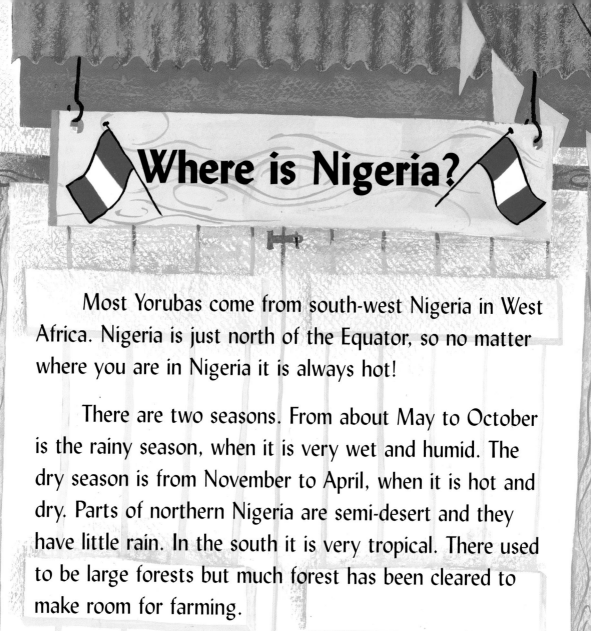

Where is Nigeria?

Most Yorubas come from south-west Nigeria in West Africa. Nigeria is just north of the Equator, so no matter where you are in Nigeria it is always hot!

There are two seasons. From about May to October is the rainy season, when it is very wet and humid. The dry season is from November to April, when it is hot and dry. Parts of northern Nigeria are semi-desert and they have little rain. In the south it is very tropical. There used to be large forests but much forest has been cleared to make room for farming.

The capital city of Nigeria is Abuja. It is in the very middle of the country. The main port and trading centre is Lagos.

Niger

Chad

KANO

NIGERIA

JOS

Benin

Niger River

ABUJA

OYO

IBADAN • OSOGBO

ABEOKUTA

LAGOS

Cameroon

Atlantic Ocean

equator

Africa

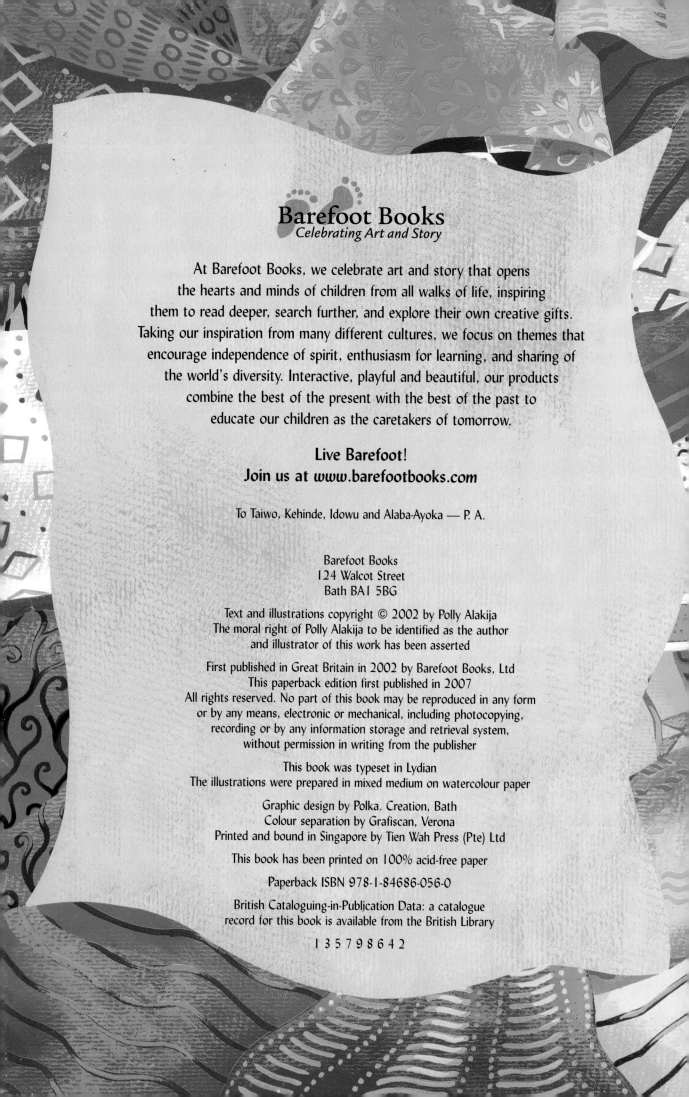

Barefoot Books
Celebrating Art and Story

At Barefoot Books, we celebrate art and story that opens
the hearts and minds of children from all walks of life, inspiring
them to read deeper, search further, and explore their own creative gifts.
Taking our inspiration from many different cultures, we focus on themes that
encourage independence of spirit, enthusiasm for learning, and sharing of
the world's diversity. Interactive, playful and beautiful, our products
combine the best of the present with the best of the past to
educate our children as the caretakers of tomorrow.

Live Barefoot!
Join us at www.barefootbooks.com

To Taiwo, Kehinde, Idowu and Alaba-Ayoka — P. A.

Barefoot Books
124 Walcot Street
Bath BA1 5BG

Text and illustrations copyright © 2002 by Polly Alakija
The moral right of Polly Alakija to be identified as the author
and illustrator of this work has been asserted

This book was typeset in Lydian
The illustrations were prepared in mixed medium on watercolour paper

Graphic design by Polka. Creation, Bath
Colour separation by Grafiscan, Verona
Printed and bound in Singapore by Tien Wah Press (Pte) Ltd

This book has been printed on 100% acid-free paper

Paperback ISBN 978-1-84686-056-0

British Cataloguing-in-Publication Data: a catalogue
record for this book is available from the British Library

1 3 5 7 9 8 6 4 2